JUST LIKE SOFT FRUIT

DANI TAUBER

*...IS THE WAY I LICK
HONEY OFF A
SPOON
51
YOU GOT
NOTHING FROM
ME
52
LATE(LY)
BLOOM(ING)
53
ISOLATED VOCAL
TRACK
54
SENSORY MEMORY
55
SOMETIMES THIS
SHIT GETS REALLY
REAL
56
LA PETITE MORT
57
ONE OF MY MORE
PLEASANT
FAILURES
58
THREE TRUE
THINGS
59
PLEASE COME
TRUE
60
PUT OUT
61
VULNERARIES
62
AT SOME POINT
EVERYTHING WILL
GO TOO FAR
63
NEVER. GET. RID.
64
THINGS I DO NOT
DESERVE
65*

To decay, soft rot, and dust.

DOWRY

a perfect mouth. big eyes.
magic tricks learned in
back seats on hot nights,
in teenage bedrooms, on
weekend vacations in
cheap motels. a daring
topless photo, taken in
direct sunlight, in which i
look like an actual angel.

UNTITLED

you and i facing each
other in bed, our
knees touching; you
try to wipe my tears
away but they just
keep on coming and
we both wish we were
fucking instead.

TURNS OUT I HAD JUST
BEEN CONSUMED

and although you were the devil
i felt holy in your bed - more
than half asleep on a lazy sunday
morning, hungover and almost
almost-touching but still feeling
as though something had been
consummated; a fire stoked,
somewhere.

UNTITLED

i cried in your bed and a
tiny seed of doubt sprouted
from your dirty sheets;
the berries looked toxic.
i ate them anyway.
there was pie all summer.

AUTOBIOGRAPHICAL

i am the human embodiment
of a roadside memorial -
beautiful and tragic all at once.

i am the human embodiment
of water in a bathtub -
immediately unconcerning but
still deep enough to drown in.

i am the human embodiment
of that dead fern on the fire
escape at your apartment -
you could have tried harder.
but you didn't.

RIPE

she was like a ghost in a
fever dream that could only be
seen in glimpses through the
august blur; fingers by her mouth,
picking at the dry skin of her
perfect chapped lips. her thin
dress stuck to her thighs and
when she readjusted the hem
she left a small smearing of
blood on the white cotton.
the same blood dripped down
her chin, wiped away without
much thought with the back of
a hand like the juice of some
beautiful fruit no one could
pronounce the name of.
they couldn't pronounce hers,
either; they didn't know it.
they just knew she was in bloom.

OH YES I DID MEAN IT LITERALLY
WHEN I SAID THIS WOULD
KILL YOU SOMEDAY

all those nights when the
heat in your jeans couldn't
stop your shivering and
my tongue was like medicine -
you still think about it
because it still matters and
you could pick up the phone
but you don't. throat's sore
from not talking about it.
head aches from the needing.
your hands shake because
they miss being in my hair,
and you could just die over it.

BUT YOU'RE GONNA LEAVE
WITH NOTHING

i look up at you from the floor
with my mouth open and hungry,
tongue purple from candy and you
think, oh my god, this is it, this
is everything, and it is. it is.

UNTITLED

like a canary in a
coal mine my mouth
only opens for
total devastation -
be it words or tongue
or both. you lay
back like neither
of us knows what
happens next.

THE THREE OF US IN
AN INTIMATE SETTING

you and me and my
overwhelming desire
to get to know as much
about you as possible
while still keeping you
an arm's length away.

AND YOU KNOW
THERE'S SOME THINGS
THAT WATER CAN'T WASH CLEAN -
YOU'RE GONNA NEED GASOLINE

you had me and then you
didn't - let me slip through
your careless fingers and then
through a crack in the sidewalk,
down your shower drain. you
wash your hands until they're
raw; until they crack and bleed.
but i'm still under your fingernails.

UNTITLED

we wound up at the
same party and you
looked good and you
brushed up against me
on your way back out
of my life; sent fucking
sparks up my spine and
i collapsed. i was fucking
paralyzed on that floor
for hours. people spilled
their beers all over my
dress, stepped on my face.
i'd started collecting dust.

THE PAIN IS UNIMAGINABLE

you pin my hips to the
mattress underneath you like
an insect to a bit of cork;
you pull the wings right off
my back with your teeth.

UNTITLED

his hand slides between
my thighs cold as ice
against my fire; i am the
apple as well as the snake.

SCRAPS

I.
i'm so fucking heavy that i am
amazed every time i lay down
on the floor and don't just
crash right through it.

II.
i'm not numb enough,
i'm not numb enough,
i'm not numb enough.

III.
i'm fucked hard against a wall
by denial while want and need
take turns helping each other
purge in the bathroom.

FORGIVE ME IF AT FIRST I BITE

take me in like the wounded,
dying animal that i am -
feed me. bathe me, clean
me up. stitch what needs
stitching, bandage the rest.
scrub away years of abuse
and neglect to find me.
give me someplace soft
and warm and safe to sleep.
show me kindness for the
first time in my life; approach
me with your gentle hands
visible and open, palms out.

GIRLHOOD

my lips were the colour of
poisonous berries but you
kissed them anyway; the
summer was a fever, air
heavy and thick, dizzy on
the stench of rotting fruit.
horrid and sweet. your
little bruised peach; you
put your hands on me
in the grass behind your
house and i let you.
two years older, okay,
count my bug bites.
tell me i'll grow into my
clumsy smile. five years
from now the sound of
ice in a glass will still
make me terribly uneasy.

*TO BLOSSOM IS TO BEGIN
TO DECAY*

when we are of age, we birth
our biggest mistakes. nurture
our worst regrets. lay down
for sons and fathers who
don't know how to hold us
but know how our mouths
are supposed to feel to them,
how our bodies are supposed
to please them, blossom for them
and oh, there is so much blood.

YOU WISH YOU KNEW

the soft sounds that
spill from my mouth in
dimly lit bedrooms and
high socks and fingertips
and tip-toes and cloves
and i've sewn black bows
onto the backs of all my
black under-things, too.

A PLACE YOU'D WANT TO VISIT
OFTEN

your cheeks flushed, your chest…
eyelids so heavy they just
stopped trying, panting and
sweating, your hair fell into
your face and you looked
like you had just been born
and i had too. i had, too…
glowing in the aftermath,
searching for our underwear.
i left my old skin at your
house, kicked it under your
bed while you were in the
bathroom. didn't recognize
this pale, glistening, wild-
haired waif in the mirror
over your desk, watching me
as i emptied a lifetime of self
doubt into one of the drawers,
as i spat shyness out of an
open window. i gave her a
little twirl; so this is me, now.
this body used to be a prison.
now it's a playground with a
garden. a fountain. the
greenest grass you've ever seen.

I'VE NEVER HAD A GARDEN BEFORE

life took its fists
to all of my softest parts
and i took mine
to my bedroom wall.
couldn't eat for days after;
crooked fingers couldn't
grasp a sandwich, a spoon.
on the fourth day
i ate dry toast and
with a marker, drew
stems and leaves
beneath the dark spots
left by my breaking knuckles.
i had dozens of flowers to
look after now. exhausting.
i thought about making
lemonade but couldn't
get up off the floor.

I AM A WAR

i wish i was a bombshell but
i am just the shrapnel, caught
in your side that keeps you
up and in pain at night. and
you sleep next to my body
like broken glass and have
flashbacks to soft skin and
long hair that smells sweet
like strawberries and cream.

*ALWAYS LEAVING LITTLE PIECES
OF MYSELF EVERYWHERE*

i walk in and take off my
dress. i start to cut up
an onion and slice off the
tip of my finger, blood all over;
was smart to take off the dress.
i cough teeth up into the sink.
strands of hair on pillows,
eyelashes in my milk.
a barrette on the sidewalk.
a button, a receipt, a ribbon.
according to the state of my
lipstick, i left my mouth
around his dick and i don't
think i'm gonna get it back.

*IT'S OKAY IF IT TURNS YOU ON
A LITTLE*

sometimes i will need you to
hold me down -
sometimes i will need to feel
weight on top of me
that isn't my own.

UNTITLED

after several days and nights
of not being able to talk about
myself without crying and
several more days and nights of
just crying, i woke up with an
insatiable fever.

it was august and
the flames sought to
consume everything.

my hair was damp and matted;
the bed sheets clung to the
backs of my legs. too hot for
under-things, the white dress
i put on to leave the house
was slick and see-through
within minutes. i left my shoes.

i don't know how long i walked.
i don't remember exactly when
it started raining. but i guess it did.

he called to me from his
front steps - "baby it's raining!
come inside." i paused. i said,
"it's alright." he said, "oh, honey."

and then very suddenly, his fingers
were wrapped tight around my
arm and i was following him up
the driveway. up the steps.
like a lamb to the slaughter,
into his house. "it's warm in here."
i said, "i'm too warm." he said,
"come warm up in here,
sit right here."

the couch was gray and
dusty and uncomfortable.
i made note of every exit but
i was tired from walking so
i didn't run. he brought me
hot tea but i couldn't drink it.
my throat felt like cigarette ash.

he said, "oh sweetie, we have to
get these knots out of your hair!"
he pulled at it. hard.

he put his thumb between my lips.
he did not look me in the eye.
he said, "oh angel, we have to
get you out of these soaked clothes!"
he pulled down the top of my dress.
hard. the coals in my rib cage

flushed my bare chest bright red.

"oh!" he said. "like a robin!
how pretty! so pretty. you're pretty!"
he touched me without asking.
he said, "i'll keep you. i want you.
i need you. i have to have you."

it seemed like forever, his hand
around my throat. the other
up my dress. it took only seconds
for the flames to leap to his
face, his hair. the couch,
the carpet. my blood boiled. the skin
of his horrid hands bubbled.

i preferred his screaming
to his sweet talk. i fixed
my dress and started walking
back in the opposite direction.
until i was home, back in bed.

i read in the papers later that
the smoke could be seen for miles.
there was nothing left of the house.
he died horribly and painfully.

i think i am wanted for
arson in the state of new jersey.
i think his name was james.
i think i am starting to feel better.

VIEW FROM ABOVE

i've got a face that
just screams, hurt me;
delicate features that
practically beg for bruises
and a haunting stare that
draws even the gentlest
hands to my throat.

MAYBE I'LL BURN DOWN AND GROW
BACK NEW LIKE A TINY FOREST
BUT PROBABLY NOT

the air is thick and hot and
heavy; i smell someone's bonfire
through an open window and
it mixes with the patchouli incense
my father lit. my lungs are wet
tissue paper; they stick. my
throat is coated with soot.
maybe it will all go up in flames.

scratch at the soft skin of your
thigh until it peels and bleeds -
continue until the wound is large
enough for you to fold up into
yourself and disappear completely.

TINY CRIES

my own voice sounds
strange to me, after
so many years with
your hand at my throat.

LIMP ALONG

i was not born graceful enough to
be a knife thrower's assistant
and yet life keeps tossing; i didn't
always move this slow. i'm just in a lot of
fucking pain.

RUB MY BACK

after major spinal surgery,
it can take five, ten, fifteen years
for some nerves to fully regenerate.
your fingertips feel different each time.

IT BITES MY LIPS UNTIL THEY BLEED

the weight of being
sits on my chest at
night, covers my mouth
with cold hands. it
licks the salt off my
face when i cry; it
gets fat off my misery.

*HOW DARE YOU LOOK AT ME AND
ASSUME I MUST BE STARVING?*

you felt like warm,
heavy ash on my
tongue; like sand
down my throat.

PRESSURE

head's goddamn heavy.
heart's goddamn heavy.
soul's goddamn…i get up
out of bed in the morning
and sometimes my ankle
cracks and sometimes it's
so fucking loud, just like
lightning tearing through
an old dead tree and it

scares me.

HIC…

i start hiccuping and excitedly i think
oh god, oh shit, what if my heart just
stops?! and then i think, oh no, oh fuck,
what if it doesn't?

I'VE HEARD FEELING THINGS
CAN BE NICE AND I NEED PROOF

just shove me hard against a wall
so i can feel something; even if
it's just a bruised shoulder or a
mild concussion.

*THERE IS SOMETHING VERY
WRONG WITH YOU*

and eventually it will get so bad that you'll
reach the point where there are no tears
streaming down your face as you stand
in the shower, just the steaming hot water
that softens the fingernails you drag across
your stomach. you won't bleed. you won't
cry out. you won't feel anything. but you'll
still be something. and it won't feel right.
because it isn't.

MOTHERFUCKING DEMOLISHED

i want to punch a wall so hard and
with such rage, such force, that
something inside me splinters. i
want broken, bloody knuckles and
exposed bone, i want the outsides
to match the insides, and i want to
shed not one tear on the way to
the emergency room. and i want
the nurse to look at me, this 5'2",
94 pound waif of a girl, practically
nothing, and the damage i have
done, and i want her to be terrified.

men take me into their arms, and are
surprised by how light i am. how soft.
and then my mouth opens and the
flood comes and they think they'll die
unless they plug the dam; with tongues.
with fingers, with…

JUST LIKE SOFT FRUIT

i'm clumsy and my thighs are
bruised like peaches left in the
bowl a day or two too long but
i promise i'm still sweet so go on,
bite in.

I AM 28 YEARS OLD

no flowers will grow from my
rotting body and i know this
because they should have
started already.

...IS THE WAY I LICK HONEY OFF A
SPOON

intimacy is comparing the
size of our hands, is helping
me into or out of a dress,
is clasping a necklace for me
as i hold my hair out of
the way, is laying on the
couch in your arms, is that
mischievous smile you've got.

YOU GOT NOTHING FROM ME

you didn't know
my body from a
fucking hole in
the ground so
stop telling your
friends you did.

LATE(LY) BLOOM(ING)

how surreal it is, to
suddenly now know
yourself as approximately
ten perfect handfuls *
and a mouth to beg for
when you used to not
care to know yourself
in the least bit at all.

*(hips, ass, chest, throat, hair;
wrists, with just one hand,
or both).

ISOLATED VOCAL TRACK

my silence feels like an
impossible peach pit at
the back of my throat, and
tastes like the grape cough
medicine i choked down
as a sick child. i have to remind
myself to speak when i am
spoken to. i slam two fingers
in a car door and don't realize
for several seconds because
i do not cry out in pain. my
tongue eats itself alive.

SENSORY MEMORY

he gets hard in the
supermarket, thinking
about how i used to
eat spaghetti.

SOMETIMES THIS SHIT
GETS REALLY REAL

i get heartsick looking
at home and decorating
inspo photos because
nothing has ever felt
like home to me.

the longest i have ever
spent waiting for someone
to realize they love me
is three years, five months,
thirteen days; i only gave
up because i was dying.

i run my fingertips along
the curves and lines of
my body that no one touches;
i am soft enough, malleable.

every now and then when
meeting someone new for
the first time i casually mention
that i know exactly what my
last meal will be and gauge
their reaction to decide whether
or not i'll ever text them.

LA PETITE MORT

oh, to be young and
drowning in lust -
i can breathe just
fine with your hand
at my throat or
your fingers in my
mouth but i die
every time you
get out of bed.

ONE OF MY MORE
PLEASANT FAILURES…

i kissed you hard on the mouth for the
first time and you couldn't stop laughing -
i kissed you again. and again. and you
apologized. you said you weren't used to
being this way, being happy. you had
no idea what to do with yourself. i just had
this effect on you, like the nitrous oxide
when you got your wisdom teeth removed
and i kissed you again and again and
you got higher and higher on me and i'm
really sorry about the brain damage.

THREE TRUE THINGS

my chest blushes
bright red like a robin
when i am overwhelmed
or turned on.

-

i know exactly
what i am
capable of.

-

i am approximately
ten perfect
handfuls.

PLEASE COME TRUE

i lick the sweat that
pools between your
collarbones and taste
your desperation like
salt and a dry red
wine and tobacco and
maybe we're both dreaming
of the same things.

PUT OUT

before you, i'd never stood
next to such a big fire -
i threw myself on you,
i was consumed; i grew
back new, but damaged.
they say i'm lucky to have
survived; i'm alive and
i'm expected to be grateful
for it but everyone who
looks at me only sees you.

VULNERARIES

i can still see the bruises
from careless hands that
haven't touched me in years.
the cuts and scrapes all
still sting in a hot bath,
still sting after the water
has gone cold. i pick the
scabs on dates and in
bed with these dates and
on my bedroom floor and
in the space between the
bathtub and the toilet.
the old wounds still ooze -
i feel them underneath
my pretty clothes. bone
fractures and re-sets
still ache; cracked teeth,
long fixed, still feel
jagged, and so i write.
i write salves and balms
and blue pills and pink pills.
i write clean, black sutures.

AT SOME POINT, EVERYTHING
WILL GO TOO FAR

for years i laid on my
stomach in your bed as
you balanced the sharp
point of your grandfather's
pocket knife between
my shoulder blades -
you never once drew
blood. until you did.

NEVER. GET. RID.

i had my secrets, too.
should i die before him,
his best friend knows to
braid my hair, cut the
braid off at its base,
coil it tightly, and slip
it into his pillowcase
like a fucking snake.
to dilute his whiskey
with my blood, to
grind my bones to
dust and stash them
in his sugar bowl, his
salt shaker. to toss
a handful of my toe-
nails and fingernails
into each carpeted
room of his house
for him to step on,
with bare feet, forever.
to melt my lipsticks
on his radiator. and
he will, in secret.
because he was
my best friend, too.

THINGS I DO NOT DESERVE

things that i saved from the
blazing inferno that was us /
things that are too heavy to
carry / things that are too
heavy to put down / things
like shards of glass that cut
up my palms and between my
fingers / things i have swallowed
like fucking horse tranquilizers /
things that still make me nauseous
when i think about them.

Thanks must be given to Kinsey for helping me sift through and compile this absolute nightmare, Lauren for teaching me how loud to make my voice and which direction to start shouting in, Jessi for painting my insides perfectly, and Freddy for understanding completely.

Dani Tauber is a basket-case poet, professional ghost, former music journalist, and antiques archivist from NJ. She shares a room with more than 50 journals and several antique locks of hair. Her work has been published by V.A.P. and APEP Publications, and appeared in Resurrection Mag and Pink Plastic Press. She doesn't know what she's mourning yet, but she's beyond consolation.